To my mother, Kathleen BJH

To Michelle & Jennifer SM

Library of Congress Cataloging-in-Publication Data
Heinz, Brian J., 1946–
The monsters' test / by Brian J. Heinz ; pictures by Sal Murdocca.
p. cm.
Summary: Goblins, ghosts, gargoyles, and other creepy creatures
have a contest to see who is the scariest of all.
ISBN 0-7613-0050-3 (lib. bdg.). —ISBN 0-7613-0095-3 (trd. bdg.)
[1. Monsters—Fiction. 2. Halloween—Fiction. 3. Contests—
Fiction. 4. Stories in rhyme.] I. Murdocca, Sal, ill. II. Title.
PZ8.3.H41344Mo 1996
[E]—dc20 95-45477 CIP AC

Published by The Millbrook Press, Inc.
2 Old New Milford Road, Brookfield, Connecticut 06804

THE MONSTERS' TEST

BY BRIAN J. HEINZ

SCARY PICTURES BY SAL MURDOCCA

The Millbrook Press • Brookfield, Connecticut

Ten thousand dreams or more ago,
When nightmares came to be,
The Monsters' Test was waged one chilling
Moonlit Hallowe'en.
   Banshees, Ghosts, and Hags took flight—
   Gargoyles, Goblins, Poltergeists—
   And Creepy Beasties of the night
   That give one cause to scream.

It was a proper monsters' bash
Within the haunted manse.
Witches, Trolls, and Giants, too,
Were summoned to the dance.
The Zombies growled, "We're scariest."
The Dragons roared, *"We* frighten best!"
"Such silly twits!" the Imps protest.
"You couldn't scare an *aunt*."

The arguments exploded 'til the
Boogyman decreed,
"Settle down! We'll have a contest!"
They reluctantly agreed.

Each he or she, or thing or it,
Drew lots and formed a line.
And those who couldn't be the first?
They cried and stomped and whined.
The shriveled white-haired Warlock stressed,
"I'm nasty . . . frightful! I'm the best
At scaring boys and girls. Oh, yes!
I'll have those kiddies cryin'."

Thunder rumbled — lightning flashed —
He conjured up a storm.
Within the vaulted stony walls
A swollen rain cloud formed.
It poured upon the Warlock's head,
Snake eyes, bugs, and spider webs.

The Gremlins laughed. The Werewolf said,
"It's someone else's turn."
The flustered Warlock slinked away as
The Pooka held its nose,
While Trolls all smirked and snickered,
"Number two? Be on your toes!"

The bearded toothy Hag arose,
She saddled up her broom,
And buzzed the quaking monsters as she
Swooped around the room.
  She cackled while her runny nose
  Dripped upon her moldy toes and
  Plucked her hairy warts at those
  Who claimed that she would lose.

The Witch ran out of flying space and
Plummeted into the fireplace.
The Vampire howled at her disgrace!
"Number three! Please show your face."

The Banshee wailed her graveyard song
To show how she could scare.
"My spooky, shrieking, haunting voice
Can curl a bald man's hair."
She echoed 'cross the misty bogs,
The pond *ker-plooshed* with fainting frogs,
Who passed out on their resting logs, but . . .
Not one monster cared.

The Banshee lost her pride, which sent her
Hooting in a wild-eyed temper.
"I'm number four!" the Ogre bellowed,
"Step aside for a gruesome fellow."

The Ogre thumped his hairy chest
And belched a puff of smoke.
He rolled his one red eye around.
He snapped. He snarled. He croaked.
"My beastly breath can wake the dead.
I snatch the children from their bed
And grind their bones to make my bread.
I *really* scare the folk."

The audience was nodding off—
The Ogre's act fell flat—
And while he wept a noise burst forth.
The Goblins yelled, "What's that?"

The gathering was shaken by a
Pounding on the doors.
The Gargoyles grasped the old brass knobs
With sweating scaly paws.
　　The monsters gasped at what they saw—
　　Rapscallions! Scalawags! Ghouls galore
　　Came dashing in across the floor
　　With voices raised in one great roar . . .

"TRICK OR TREAT!

TRICK OR TREAT!"

they cried.

WELL . . .

The Mummy's wrappings came unspun,
The Wolfman lost his hair,
And Gremlins snatched at flapping bats that
Dragged them through the air.
Monsters, brutes, and horrid beasts
Beat their feet in swift retreat
And fled the house in disbelief.
They'd *never* been so scared.

The costumed children fell in laughter,
Raised their masks, and pranced.
They knew those silly, bumbling monsters
Never had a chance!

But . . .

The Monsters' Test was incomplete.
Who *had* the greatest BOO?
You'll have to pick the winner,
Unless, of course . . .